IN THE
MARGINS

PAIRED:

Two exiles who found a new home in their writing.
Sherman Alexie left the reservation to get an
education, but only poetry taught him what it
meant to be an Indian. Julia Alvarez left the
Dominican Republic for the United States
and spent decades trying to find her voice.

"I was a Spokane Indian. I belonged to that tribe. But I also belonged to the tribe of American immigrants. And the tribe of basketball players. And to the tribe of bookworms."

"I am a Dominican, *hyphen*, American.
As a writer, I find that the most exciting things
happen in the realm of that hyphen—the place
where two worlds collide or blend together."

Julia Alvarez

Photographs © 2012: Alamy Images: 88, 89 (Bertrand Gardel/Hemis), 36 (Andre Jenny), 31 (Pictorial Press), 10 (Joe Sohm/Visions of American, LLC); AP Images/Ramon Espinosa: back cover right, 3 right; Barry G. Moses: 18; Corbis Images: 54, 77 (Bettmann), 64 (Johannes Loewe); Ellen Forney, 2007: cover, 34, 35, 41, 51; Everett Collection, Inc.: 96 (Bazille/Showtime), 44, 48 (Miramax); Getty Images: back cover left, 3 left (Ulf Anderson), 69 (Robert W. Kelley/Time Life Pictures), 80 (Bob Koller/NY Daily News), 74 (Fred W. McDarrah), 52 (Anthony Pidgeon/Redferns), 12 (Rex Rystedt/Time & Life Pictures), 84 (B. Anthony Stewart/National Geographic), 83 (Stockbyte); Library of Congress/Edward S. Curtis Collection: 21; NASA/Goddard Space Flight Center/NASA's Earth Observatory: 14; NEWSCOM: 90 (KRT), 100 (Peggy Peattie/San Diego Union-Tribune/Zuma Press); ShutterStock, Inc.: cover background; Superstock, Inc.: 47 (All Canada Photos), 24 (Joe Schuster); Tamela J. Wolff: 28; The Image Works/Stuart Cohen: 61.
Illustrations by CCI: 14, 58.

Library of Congress Cataloging-in-Publication Data

Shea, John, 1966-
In the margins / John Shea.
p. cm. -- (On the record)
Includes bibliographical references and index.
ISBN-13: 978-0-531-22556-1
ISBN-10: 0-531-22556-9
1. Alexie, Sherman, 1966---Juvenile literature. 2. Indians of North America--Biography--Juvenile literature. 3. Authors, American--20th century--Biography--Juvenile literature. 4. Alvarez, Julia--Juvenile literature. 5. Hispanic American women authors--Biography--Juvenile literature. 6. Authors, American--21st century--Biography--Juvenile literature. I. Title. II. Series.

PS3551.L35774Z74 2011
818'.5409--dc22
2011003105

Tod Olson, Series Editor
Marie O'Neill, Creative Director
Curriculum Concepts International, Production
Thanks to John DiConsiglio

7 8 9 10   40   21 20 19 18

IN THE MARGINS

They found their place by not fitting in.

John Shea

Contents

NO RESERVATION

Sherman Alexie left the Spokane Indian
Reservation to get a better education. As an
American Indian in a white world, he struggled
to answer basic questions: Who am I?
And where is my true tribe?

Sherman Alexie poses for a photograph in 1995.
Alexie says he began to write when "I saw my
life in poems and stories for the very first time."

1
Between Two Tribes

Life doesn't get any better than this, Sherman Alexie thought. The ninth grader was hanging out with his new friends at a local pizza joint. He was acing his classes and starting to feel like he belonged at his new school. As they joked over sodas and slices, Sherman couldn't stop smiling at his pretty girlfriend.

He almost had to pinch himself. If this is a dream, he thought, please don't wake me up.

Spokane Reservation

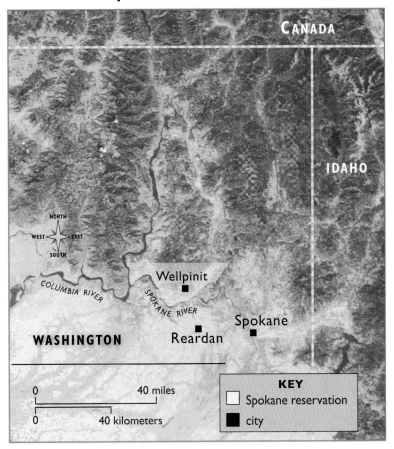

The Spokane Indians once inhabited northeastern Washington, northern Idaho and western Montana. They now live on 154,000 acres in Wellpinit, Washington.

It was 1982 in Reardan, a small farm town in eastern Washington State. And even as Sherman felt the warmth of success, he recognized a familiar twinge of anxiety. He knew he didn't really belong in this world. He wasn't from Reardan. Unlike his buddies and his girlfriend, he didn't have money in his pockets. And he wasn't white.

He was a Spokane/Coeur d'Alene Indian, and lived on the Spokane Indian Reservation. Each morning and night he made the 22-mile trip between two very different worlds.

Alexie would later describe the "rez," as it was called, as a dirt-poor landscape of "shacks and abandoned cars." Many families—including Sherman's—battled alcoholism and unemployment. His parents made so little money that sometimes his family went without dinner. The reservation school was lousy, with burned-out teachers and 30-year-old textbooks. So Sherman had transferred to Reardan High. Reardan promised a much better education, but the only other Indian at the school was the mascot.

That evening at the restaurant, Sherman faced a painful reminder of who he was and where he came from. As he laughed with his friends, an Indian man staggered into the restaurant. He steadied himself on a stool and slurred his speech, obviously drunk. The waiter ignored the man. Sherman's girlfriend leaned in and whispered, "I hate Indians." Sherman felt his face redden. His friends looked away, embarrassed.

Sherman's whole life lay ahead of him, but he would never forget that moment at the pizzeria. Sherman had longed to fit in with his white friends and break free of the reservation. But as he worked to become a writer in the years to come, he would return often to moments like this one. He would write about the many times he felt confused by his identity, caught between two cultures.

That night, as his girlfriend sneered at the drunken Indian, Sherman again asked himself the question that was never far from his mind: was he too Indian for his high school—or too white for the rez?

He would spend much of his youth working out the answers.

The Spokane Indian Reservation is bordered by the Spokane River (above). The word *Spokane* means "children of the sun" in Spokane Salish, the tribe's language.

2

On the Rez

In some ways, Alexie was born an outsider. As a baby, he suffered from a life-threatening condition called hydrocephaly—excess fluid in his skull. Doctors told his parents that they could operate to remove the fluid, but the risks were high. If Sherman survived, he would almost certainly end up with severe brain damage.

Sherman made it through the operation with his brainpower intact, but the condition made it hard to have a normal childhood. He suffered seizures until he was seven. While other boys climbed trees and chased girls, Sherman spent a lot of time by himself, observing the world around him.

The world of the Spokane people had shrunk dramatically since the time of Sherman's ancestors. For centuries, the Spokane had made their home on three million acres of land, fishing in the Spokane River and hunting in the mountains. By the 1860s, however, whites were pressing into their territory. The new settlers brought smallpox and other diseases that killed Indians by the thousands.

Eventually, U.S. soldiers forced the Spokane and other Native American tribes onto "reserved" lands to make room for white settlers. In many cases, the reservations had poor soil and few resources.

In the early 1900s, photographer Edward S. Curtis took more than 40,000 photos of about 80 Indian tribes. This Curtis photo shows Spokane Indians on horseback.

By the 1880s, the world of the Spokane had been whittled down to about 150,000 acres. The Spokane were forced to abandon their villages and burial grounds, and their population shrank.

Only in the 1960s and 1970s did Indian tribes like the Spokane begin to regain some autonomy and lost rights. But many reservations struggled with poverty, unemployment, and drug and alcohol abuse.

Sherman lived on the rez with his parents and four siblings. His father was gentle and caring, but also an alcoholic. He held a string of jobs, from truck driver to logger, but he couldn't stay sober long enough to keep them. His mother sold hand-sewn quilts. After she quit drinking, she became the reservation's only addiction counselor.

Despite their troubles, Sherman's parents passed along a love of reading and a sense of humor. As Sherman recovered from brain surgery, his father read to him from paperback Westerns and detective novels. Sherman also devoured Superman comic books. By age six, he finished the 400-plus pages of John Steinbeck's classic book *The Grapes of Wrath*.

Reading had become a way to survive. "If one reads enough books, one has a fighting chance," Alexie observes. "Or better, one's chances of survival increase with each book one reads."

Sherman was a misfit in grade school. He disappeared into his basement bedroom for all-night games of Dungeons and Dragons. His appearance made him a

When Alexie was three, he taught himself to read with a Superman comic book. Soon he was reading everything he could: "I read the backs of cereal boxes. I read the newspaper . . . I read junk mail. I read auto-repair manuals."

target for bullies. He had a big head and huge feet on a beanpole body. Kids called him a "retard" and a "hydro-head."

Sherman found ways to fight back. He was smart and did better in school than the kids who picked on him. "I was fierce in the class-room," he says. "My self-worth was related to how much I could humiliate my classmates." As Sherman earned straight As, he teased the bullies for missing answers and failing tests. His sharp tongue earned him multiple after-school beatings.

When life grew too stressful, Sherman went to the place where he felt most at home: the basketball court. The rez court had cockeyed hoops and cracked blacktop, but it was a good place to blow off steam and polish his skills. His lifelong love affair with basketball began on that court.

"I had learned to fight to live."

By age 12, Sherman had read every book in the school library, and by 13, he realized that the rez school had taught him everything it could. If he wanted to keep learning, he had to find a school that would challenge him. "I had learned to fight to live, and somehow I knew that I had to leave to live, and if I stayed, I'd die," he says.

If he was going to leave, Sherman decided, he would go to the best school he could reach—in the farm town of Reardan, 22 miles away.

Sherman knew that no one ever left the reservation, especially for school. He wasn't sure how to tell his parents that he wanted to leave. He was afraid his plans would hurt their feelings, so he was surprised when they barely blinked at the news. They recognized that this was their son's chance to follow his own path and perhaps escape the harshness of reservation life.

"They just said okay," he says, "and it didn't occur to me until years later how amazing that was because, in a sense, I did betray the tribe. I left it, but I also left my family."

Reardan is home to about 600 people. The town's schools attract students from the surrounding area. In fact, there are more students at Reardan schools than there are inhabitants in the town.

3
A Boy Called Apple

eardan High—even the name made Sherman nervous. Compared to the rez, this place felt like another world.

None of Sherman's friends back on the reservation believed he'd really go through with it. As he watched a crowd stream off the school bus in front of the school, Sherman wondered whether his old friends were right. It wasn't just that the Reardan students were all white. They wore new jeans and had cool haircuts. They had money, opportunities, and high expectations for their lives.

Overnight, Sherman's world was turned inside out. The people on the reservation considered him a traitor—an Indian acting like he was better than his people. His peers called him an "apple"—red on the outside, white on the inside. Sometimes they beat him up.

At his new school, Sherman faced the challenge of being a new kid and the only Indian. He braced himself for insults from whites, both in school and around town. "There was a lot of random racial slurring growing up . . . in eastern Washington," he says.

Sherman was accustomed to being at the top of his class, but even that was not a sure thing at Reardan. His new classmates seemed to be out of his league. Many were looking ahead to college. He didn't know

When Alexie was a boy, one of the best-known portrayals of a Native American was Tonto from the TV show *The Lone Ranger.* Tonto was brave and dependable, but his name revealed prejudices of the day. The Spanish word *tonto* means "stupid."

"Keep my mouth shut and be a good Indian."

how he could fit in, let alone compete. He resolved to "keep my mouth shut and be a good Indian," he says.

That meant doing the same things that his white classmates did. He went out for the basketball team and was shocked when he made the varsity squad. He joined the debate team. He was elected class president.

He impressed people with his sharp sense of humor. Before long he was dating a popular girl in school. He excelled in his classes. Sherman began to realize he had the ability and opportunity to go where no one in his family had gone before—to college.

He rarely talked about his home life with his white friends, but tragedies on the reservation continued to haunt him. His dad would go on drinking binges and disappear for several days at a time. Drunk-driving accidents claimed friends and acquaintances. His sister died when her trailer caught fire and the smoke alarm failed to wake her from a drunken sleep.

The more heartbreak he experienced on the reservation, the more Sherman withdrew into his world at Reardan High.

Fitting in wasn't always easy. His basketball teammates drove their own cars to their middle-class homes with neatly trimmed lawns. Sherman rode the bus to the end of the line and sometimes had to hitchhike the final five miles home. Eventually, a Reardan family let him stay with them so he wouldn't have to make the long trip to and from the rez. But he could never shake the feeling that he was an intruder in both worlds.

As graduation approached, Sherman was still conflicted. He was popular at Reardan and had become a star athlete and top student. Shouldn't he be the pride of his people on the reservation? Or would he always be an outcast? Was it time to return to his tribe, or to flee even further from it?

This illustration is from Alexie's book *The Absolutely True Diary of a Part-Time Indian.*

Alexie attended Gonzaga University for two years before transferring to Washington State University.

4
Reservation of the Mind

During his senior year in high school, Sherman was offered a scholarship to Gonzaga University in Spokane, Washington. He would be one of the few Indians from his reservation to attend college, and he felt the weight of expectations. "I had a whole tribe waiting for me to fail or not fail—and some were doing both," he says.

It wasn't long before his old identity crisis crept back in. Gonzaga was like Reardan High—only bigger with even more pressure. And the freedom of college life was a shock for him. "I was utterly confused when I got there," he says.

Alexie grew depressed and lonely, and he cracked under the strain. He had tried to avoid drinking during high school, knowing how much damage it had done to his family and friends on the reservation, but now alcohol became his comfort. He threw himself into a life of binge drinking and college parties and slept through many of his classes. "I guess I was just a lot more confident as a 16-year-old than I was as a 19-year-old," he says. "I was scared [and] alcohol numbs fears."

There was one class, however, that kept him awake. In an English literature course, Alexie found himself drawn to poetry. Bleary-eyed from long nights of drinking, he slumped in his chair and flipped through pages of John Keats, William Butler Yeats, Emily Dickinson, and Walt Whitman.

At first, Alexie found little connection between his life and the writing of these famous poets. But the more he read, the more he felt a bond with these "dead white guys," as he puts it. In their lines, Alexie found feelings of isolation and rejection, as well as fierce attempts to make sense of the world.

These poets were outcasts, just like him. "I realized I wasn't the only freak," he says.

Still, poetry did not save him from self-destruction—at least not right away. He left Gonzaga after two years and moved to Seattle, where he worked in a sandwich shop. He continued to drink heavily, and he gained a lot of weight.

He tried college again at Washington State University, where he considered pursuing a career as a doctor. But he soon found out that he couldn't stand the sight of blood. Several fainting spells in anatomy class sent him looking for another major.

Alexie enrolled in a poetry-writing class, but he spent a lot of time doodling in his note-book. He was on the verge of dropping out again and retreating in failure to the rez.

Then the words of a poem hit him with a powerful insight. A writing teacher had loaned him an anthology of Native American poetry. While reading the poem "Elegy for the Forgotten Oldsmobile" by Adrian C. Louis, Alexie was struck by a line: "I am in the reservation of my mind."

Suddenly, Alexie found himself gasping for breath. He read the line again and again.

In Alexie's book *The Absolutely True Diary of a Part-Time Indian,* the main character is a Native American teenager named Arnold Spirit Jr. Arnold often draws self-portraits (like this one) that reflect his state of mind.

It seemed to express something vital to his survival. Much of the pain he felt had to do with the real tragedies he had grown up with, but he recognized that some of it was in his mind—from the negative stereotypes of Indians in movies and history books, and from his own limited expectations for himself. "I started crying," he says. "That was my whole life."

After reading that line, he started writing poems. He wrote about the reservation and about Reardan. He wrote about his father. He wrote about how hard it was to be an Indian in a white world.

Alexie kept drinking, but he also kept pouring words onto paper. He sent poem after poem to literary magazines and, like most writers, got rejection after rejection.

In 1991, Alexie hit rock bottom, blacking out after a night of heavy drinking. He realized he had to make a change. Alcoholism had plagued his family and his people for generations. Now it threatened to destroy him. He vowed to quit drinking for good.

The very next day, he received the news he had been waiting for. His first book of poetry, *The Business of Fancydancing*, had been accepted for publication. It was "a powerful coincidence," he says. He put down the bottle and hasn't touched it since.

Evan Adams (left) and Adam Beach starred in the 1998 movie *Smoke Signals.* Alexie wrote the screenplay based on stories from his book *The Lone Ranger and Tonto Fistfight in Heaven.*

5
Walking Tall

By 1994, Alexie had published five books of poetry and an award-winning book of short stories, *The Lone Ranger and Tonto Fistfight in Heaven*. He had left Washington State before graduating, but his books sold well enough for him to become a full-time writer. In 1995, officials at Washington State reviewed their records and realized that Alexie had, in fact, completed his requirements. They awarded him his degree.

Alexie discovered an emotional and spiritual outlet in his writing. He compared it to "fancy dancing," a colorful, energetic Indian dance style. Alexie even used the term in the title of his first book of poetry, *The Business of Fancydancing.*

Alexie's teenage experiences often spilled into his writing. His Indian characters battle alcoholism, prejudice, self-hatred, and powerlessness, and sometimes they make a mess of their lives. They are sad and angry, but they're also tough, brave, and wickedly funny, like their creator. Alexie has woven some of these stories into stand-up comedy routines.

Alexie's writing has offended more than a few Indian readers. Old friends and acquaintances have accused him of making fun of Indians and focusing on their faults.

This fancy dancer is a member of the Blackfoot people. Fancy dancing was developed in the 1930s. It's loosely based on traditional dances performed before battle.

Alexie's *Smoke Signals* was the first major film written, directed, and acted by Native Americans. Here, 31-year-old Alexie (right) meets on the set with director Chris Eyre, a Cheyenne/Arapaho Indian.

As a librarian on the Spokane Indian Reservation told the *New York Times Magazine*, "He has wounded a lot of people, and a lot of people feel he should try to write something positive."

Alexie says he celebrates Indian culture—faults and all. He wouldn't be telling the truth, he insists, if he ignored issues like alcoholism and poverty.

In 2007, Alexie published *The Absolutely True Diary of a Part-Time Indian*. It's an irreverent and moving novel, partially based on his childhood and adolescence. It won the National Book Award for young people's literature.

As he wrote that book, Alexie relived the most painful moments of his youth—his father's drinking, being bullied on the rez, his feelings of isolation and loneliness—

and he also remembered the positive experiences that helped him survive. In the process, he found where he truly belonged.

Near the end of *The Absolutely True Diary of a Part-Time Indian*, that hard-won discovery is shared by Arnold Spirit Jr., the book's narrator and Alexie's alter ego. "I was a Spokane Indian," Arnold says. "I belonged to that tribe. But I also belonged to the tribe of American immigrants. And the tribe of basketball players. And to the tribe of bookworms . . . It was a huge realization. And that's when I knew that I was going to be okay."

This illustration from Alexie's *The Absolutely True Diary of a Part-Time Indian* shows how the main character feels divided between two worlds.

"Humor was an antiseptic that cleaned the deepest of personal wounds," writes Sherman Alexie. He is a poet, novelist, screenwriter, director, and stand-up comedian.

Sherman Alexie

Born:

October 7, 1966

Grew up:

Spokane Indian Reservation, Washington

Life's work:

Writer and comedian

Website:

www.fallsapart.com

Favorite books include:

Ceremony, Leslie Silko

Don Quixote, Miguel de Cervantes

Howl, Allen Ginsberg

Invisible Man, Ralph Ellison

The poems of Emily Dickinson

Alexie's works include:

The Absolutely True Diary of a Part-Time Indian (novel)

The Business of Fancydancing (poetry)

I Would Steal Horses (poetry)

The Lone Ranger and Tonto Fistfight in Heaven
    (short stories)

Smoke Signals (screenplay)

War Dances (stories and poems)

One of his characters says:

"Life is a constant struggle between being an individual
and being a member of the community."

from *The Absolutely True Diary of a Part-Time Indian*

WRITING HOME

Growing up in the Dominican Republic,
Julia Alvarez dreamed of living in the
United States. When she finally got
there, she had to look back to her
homeland to find her voice.

This photograph of Julia Alvarez was taken on her farm in the Dominican Republic in 2006.

6
Escape to New York

For weeks, ten-year-old Julia Alvarez had been looking forward to her vacation. It was 1960, and trips abroad were an unusual privilege in the Dominican Republic. The government allowed only its most loyal citizens to travel outside the country.

Now, it seemed, the Alvarez family had joined the lucky few. According to their parents, Julia and her three sisters were going to the United States. Julia might even get to see snow.

Coming to America

In 1960, ten-year-old Julia Alvarez and her family
fled the Dominican Republic for New York City.

A vacation in the U.S. was an exciting prospect for Julia. She loved her Dominican home. She lived on her grandfather's estate and grew up surrounded by aunts, uncles, and cousins. But she'd always felt the pull of *el norte*—the United States.

Alvarez had been born in New York City, but her family returned to the Dominican Republic when she was just three months old. Since then her imagination had turned the U.S. into a fantasyland. "There were magical things there like snow and lots of toys lining the street," she recalls.

But even while Julia dreamed of going to the U.S., there were signs that this was no ordinary vacation. Life in the house had grown tense that year. The family hadn't made their usual summer trip to their grandfather's beach house. Julia overheard hushed conversations between her parents—in English, the language they used to keep secrets from the children. On some nights a mysterious black Volkswagen pulled into the driveway, as if to block anyone from leaving.

The family seemed to be planning for an escape, not a vacation. Suitcases had been packed for weeks while the Alvarezes waited for permission to leave, and Julia's parents had warned her not to tell anyone where they were going.

When the permission to travel finally came through, Julia's father got tickets for the next flight to New York. A parade of relatives streamed through the back door to say good-bye. And that's when the truth began to sink in: This was no vacation; they were leaving home for good.

This is a street in Santo Domingo, the capital of the Dominican Republic. The Dominican Republic shares the island of Hispaniola with the nation of Haiti and has a population of about ten million people.

Years later, Alvarez would write about that night, long after the details had faded into a blur. There was a storm rolling in and a tense wait at the airport. Her parents spoke in worried tones while she and her sisters fell asleep. The girls woke briefly to board the plane and then nodded off again.

Alvarez would remember a rush of conflicting feelings. She was excited to be moving to the place she had dreamed about for so long, but she couldn't stop thinking about the life she was leaving behind—the ocean waves outside her grandfather's beach house, the comfort of a huge extended family.

In her new home, she would pursue a different life. She would devote herself to becoming a writer. But the challenges had been laid out the day her family was

"[I] put together two different ways of seeing things."

uprooted. Years later, Alvarez discovered Maxine Hong Kingston, an author who struggled to define herself as a Chinese American. Like Kingston, Alvarez says she had to figure out how to "put together two different worlds, two different languages, two different ways of seeing things."

During the dictatorship of Rafael Trujillo, the secret police traveled in black Volkswagen Beetles like this one. Dominicans knew that if a black VW appeared in their driveways, they were in danger.

7

Calm Before the Storm

Before her family's nighttime escape, Alvarez had lived a relatively sheltered life in the Dominican Republic. Her grandfather was a wealthy and respected diplomat who often traveled outside the country. The family's wealth had shrunk over the years, but they still owned a sprawling property with several houses on it. The grounds were decorated with almond trees, hibiscus, and an orchid greenhouse.

The property was big enough to house Julia's immediate family, as well as the families of aunts, uncles, and cousins. Alvarez remembers being cared for by a collection of maids and female relatives. The cousins often gathered for meals at whatever house they happened to be near.

"We were raised in a huge, loving, extended *familia*," Alvarez recalls. "It was a wonderful life—a magical life."

But life outside the compound walls was no fairy tale. For 30 years, the Dominican Republic had been suffering under the iron-fisted reign of Rafael Trujillo. To maintain power, Trujillo fixed elections and dissolved political parties. He stole land and hoarded the country's wealth. Dominicans saw their civil rights and freedoms evaporate.

Trujillo kept a suspicious eye on any potential enemies. His secret police cruised the streets in black Volkswagen Beetles,

"We grew up in a terrible dictatorship."

arresting opponents of the regime. Trujillo's political foes were taken to prisons where they were tortured and often murdered.

Julia's parents shielded her from the nation's nightmare. "We grew up in a terrible dictatorship, really scary times, and I didn't know anything about it," she says.

But Julia's father was well aware of Trujillo's brutality. As a young medical student, Eduardo Alvarez had protested against the government. He fled the Dominican Republic in 1937 when he was targeted by Trujillo's secret police. He escaped to Canada where he earned his medical license and began a career as a doctor.

Julia's mother had also left her home in the Dominican Republic. She went to a private boarding school in New England. She and Eduardo met at a party in New York City and married soon after. Neither of them thought they would ever see their home country again. In 1950, Julia was born in New York.

Around the time of Julia's birth, Trujillo announced plans to reform his government. He encouraged Dominican exiles to return home. Julia's mother had grown desperately homesick for her family, and Julia's father, wanting to make her happy, agreed to move back to their homeland.

Trujillo's secret police kept an eye on anyone suspected of questioning his leadership. Here, they raid the headquarters of an opposition political party.

Julia was just a baby, but as her parents would remind her, she would always be an American. "You could become president," her father told her. "You were born there."

Even in the Dominican Republic, Julia was surrounded by American culture. She and her sisters ate cornflakes for breakfast, bought ice cream from an American-owned store, and shopped at Mr. Wimpy's, a supermarket that sold American products.

Julia and her sisters attended a private school run by an American teacher. Each morning, the students recited the Pledge of Allegiance to the United States and sang "America the Beautiful." They learned English from U.S. textbooks. Julia came to wish she had blond hair and blue eyes like the American girls in her class.

Julia entertained her classmates by inventing stories about New York. Once she told them that snow came in many colors. "Today you would say I had a great imagination," she says, "but back then the teachers would punish me for lying." Her exasperated mother was often called to the principal's office.

Julia wasn't the only gifted storyteller in her family. At every gathering, her relatives exchanged family stories. There were tales of beautiful aunts and stories of spirits and magical spells. "It was a wonderful treat to sit there and listen," she says. "Everything I learned about timing and character and humor and balance, I learned from them."

But Julia's storybook childhood didn't last. Her father had returned to his political activities and was secretly working with other activists on a plan to overthrow Trujillo. When the black Volkswagen Beetle began to appear in the driveway, he knew his work was putting him and his family in danger.

One evening, an American friend knocked on the family's door and warned Julia's father that two of his co-conspirators had been arrested. They were now being tortured in prison. It was only a matter of time before they broke down under the pressure and told Trujillo's police about the plot.

Julia's parents had an escape plan ready. Her father spread the word that he had to fly to New York to observe heart surgery techniques. As American citizens, Julia and her older sister were free to leave. The rest of the family began the long wait for their papers.

Years later, Alvarez remembered the moment when their plane finally landed in New York. Despite all she had left behind, she was full of anticipation. "All my childhood I had longed for this moment of arrival," she writes, "and here I was, an American girl, coming home at last."

This is a Brooklyn street during the early 1960s, about the same time the Alvarez family moved to the area.

8

A New World

Julia's return to New York City was not the joyous homecoming she had imagined. Her family moved into an apartment in the borough of Brooklyn. It was a far cry from her grandfather's Dominican estate. Without all their cousins and aunts and uncles, the sisters had only each other and their parents to rely on.

Julia's fantasy of the United States fell apart. She had spent much of her young life trying to act American, but to the kids in her neighborhood and school, she was hopelessly foreign.

Julia had learned English from her American-style school in the Dominican Republic. But it hadn't prepared her for the fast-talking slang of New York. "I couldn't tell where one word ended and another began," she writes.

In the 1960s, few Dominicans lived in New York City. Although Julia and her sisters had some Puerto Rican classmates, they barely met anyone from their home country.

Their reception at school was hardly welcoming. Boys threw stones at them and told them to go back where they came from. Some students called Julia a "spic." Their mother insisted that they were asking her to "speak," but the Alvarez

Demonstrators protest against Rafael Trujillo in New York City in 1959.

sisters soon got the message: "You don't belong here."

Julia and her sisters did what they could to fit in. They straightened their hair and tried to look American. But the differences were hard to hide. Their accents were thick; their dresses were formal and out of style; the food in their lunchboxes smelled garlicky; and they laughed loudly and made enough noise at home to make their neighbors complain.

At 13, Julia's parents transferred her to a Catholic boarding school in New England. But she still had trouble making friends, and the nuns punished her for speaking Spanish at recess.

As Julia became increasingly cut off from other kids, she retreated into herself. It seemed like the America of her dreams was rejecting her. "The feeling of loss caused a radical change in me. It made me an introverted, shy little girl."

As her loneliness grew, she discovered an unlikely source of comfort: books. In the Dominican Republic, Julia had never been a reader; her family's stories were more interesting than any book she had read. But in the U.S., reading soon filled the long hours she spent by herself.

When her mother noticed Julia's newfound love of reading, she took her daughter to a branch of the New York Public Library. Julia was dumbstruck. There were rows and rows of books. Her mother explained that Julia could pick out any book and take it home with her.

Students and researchers crowd the main reading room of the New York Public Library in 1964. Alvarez's local library changed her. She found a freedom in books that she hadn't experienced before.

"Books were places where you weren't barred," Alvarez says. "There were no signs at the beginning of a book saying no blacks, no spics, no girls allowed. Anyone was welcomed in."

At first, she moved slowly through the pages, improving her English by careful reading. "Not understanding the language, I had to pay close attention to each word—great training for a writer," she writes.

Each book took her to new places in her imagination, even as she found reflections of her own life. In the Nancy Drew mysteries, she discovered a heroine who didn't let anyone stand in her way as she solved crimes. *The Swiss Family Robinson* was an adventure story about a shipwrecked family doing their best to survive all by themselves—that reminded Julia of her own family's struggle. And because she herself was one of four sisters, Julia identified with the four March sisters in the classic novel *Little Women*, who tried to keep each other's spirits up during the American Civil War.

"I had discovered this wonderful world at last," she says. "I had come searching for the United States of America—and I found it between the covers of books."

Julia discovered her true self in books. She says, "Any writer who writes a fine novel or fine book is my teacher!"

In the U.S., Julia struggled to fit in. In this 1959 photo, a homogeneous group of students start the school day by saying the Pledge of Allegiance.

9
A Portable Homeland

At 15, Julia had landed in what she now calls "a portable homeland." It wasn't the America she'd dreamed of as a child, the nation of ice cream and happy blond-haired kids. Instead she created her own world, filled with books and writing.

Outside her family's apartment, Julia obeyed the rules she'd learned in her new country. She perfected her English and let her Spanish lapse. She became a diligent student and tried to be like a traditional American girl.

But when she picked up a pen she was able to explore her Dominican past. "The Latino world was my private world," she says. "There was no place for it outside my home. But there was a place for it on paper."

In the late 1960s, Alvarez left for Connecticut College and began writing in earnest. But she struggled to find the right voice. In classes, she was fed a steady diet of English and American writers, like William Shakespeare and Walt Whitman. These were the writers she admired, and she tried her best to sound like them.

After graduation, Alvarez was offered a place at a writers' colony in Saratoga Springs, New York. The colony, known as Yaddo, offers writers a place where they can focus on their craft.

Alvarez was assigned to write in the tower room of the Yaddo mansion, and although she was happy to be there, she couldn't seem to get words on paper.

One night she sat fidgeting at her desk, desperate for inspiration that might jump-start her writing. Instead, she heard the whirr of a vacuum cleaner. Alvarez opened her door and found a housekeeper working in the hallway. She struck up a conversation with her, and the woman invited Alvarez down to the basement for coffee with her and the cook.

The more Alvarez sneaked away from her desk to chat with the mansion's house-keepers and staff, the more her writer's block melted away. Back in her tower, words began pouring out of her. She didn't have to write like Shakespeare or Whitman;

The Playa Dorada is one of many beaches in the Dominican Republic. As Alvarez began to write,

she could capture the voice of her child-hood housekeeper gossiping and singing in the kitchen. She could describe the chirping of crickets as she and her sisters slept on the porch at their beach house. She could fill the page with the sounds of her mother and aunts laughing as they

she recalled the sights and sounds of her homeland.
She also remembered stories from family gatherings.

cooked or ironed or spread linen sheets over the children's beds. She could even retell her grandmother's stories.

"There was all this wonderful culture and background I had, which were things to tell stories about," she says, "not things to leave out."

Julia Alvarez published the novel *Before We Were Free* in 2004. It tells the story of a girl who left the Dominican Republic for New York City.

10
Migrant Poet Finds a Home

Alvarez quickly learned that it's not easy to make a living as a writer. Although she regularly published essays and poems in magazines and small literary journals, she didn't make much money as an author. She traveled across the country, taking whatever literary jobs she could find. "I was a migrant poet," she says.

In 15 years, Alvarez lived at 18 different addresses. She taught creative writing to children in Kentucky, to bilingual students in Delaware, and to senior citizens in North Carolina. She taught at colleges in California, Vermont, Washington, D.C., and Illinois. As she moved from place to place, her car rusted so badly that she could see the road through a hole in the floorboard.

Her sisters and cousins urged her to quit. "What you need is to marry a rich Dominican," one cousin advised. But Alvarez never stopped writing; every day, she'd sit at her typewriter from the moment she woke until 3:00 in the afternoon—later if she didn't have a class to teach.

"I kept reminding myself of that famous remark about writing attributed to

Hemingway," she writes. "It's one percent talent, 99 percent applying the seat of the pants to the seat of the chair."

At long last, Alvarez's determination was rewarded. In 1991, she published her first novel, *How the García Girls Lost Their Accents*, the story of four sisters who move from the Dominican Republic to New York City. The García girls struggle to find their place in a new culture, much like the Alvarez sisters had. They mimic American girls by ironing out their curls and trying to erase their accents. The book follows their lives as they rebel against their parents, fight over boyfriends, marry, and divorce. Through it all, the unbreakable bonds of their large Dominican *familia* help them survive.

Alvarez was 41 when the book was published. She had been working as a writer for more than 20 years, and she had finally broken through. *García Girls* was a hit, selling hundreds of thousands of copies. One critic praised it as "a brilliant debut."

At first, Alvarez's family wasn't so pleased with her debut. Her mother worried that people would think the book was about their family. Alvarez recalls assuring her it was fiction. "What do you mean—it's a family with four girls," her mother replied. "We have four girls. What, do you think I'm dumb?"

Even though *García Girls* was a novel, Alvarez says she had done something unusual for a Dominican woman—she had spoken out in a very public way. "Women weren't expected to have much of a public voice," she says. It was their job to guard the stories told around the dinner table and keep them within the family.

Still, Alvarez kept writing about her homeland. In 1994, she published *In the Time of the Butterflies*, a novel about the Mirabals, four real-life sisters who led an important part of the resistance movement in the Dominican Republic. Three of them were murdered by Trujillo's thugs.

When Alvarez told her mother she was working on the story, her mother was appalled. Trujillo had been dead for more than three decades, but Alvarez's mother still worried that the dictator's followers would come after the family.

The four Mirabal sisters were opponents of the Trujillo regime. Three of them were assassinated in 1960. The Mirabals were the subjects of Alvarez's 1994 book, *In the Time of the Butterflies*. It was made into a movie starring Salma Hayek (above).

When Alvarez finished the novel, she sent a copy to her mother—and hoped for the best. Her mother called within a few days, having already read the book; sobbing, she told Alvarez it had brought her right back to those days. "I don't care what happens to us!" she said. "I'm so proud of you for writing this book."

Alvarez has gone on to write many more novels, as well as poetry collections, picture books, and works of nonfiction. Along with such writers as Sandra Cisneros *(The House on Mango Street)* and Cristina García *(Dreaming in Cuban)*, she has helped bring popular attention to Latina writers in the United States.

But Alvarez doesn't like to be pigeonholed as a "Latina" writer. "It misses the point of why we tell stories," she says. "It's to connect with each other and realize we are one and the same."

In the late 1990s, Alvarez made an important connection with her homeland. With her husband, Bill Eichner, she started a coffee plantation in the Dominican Republic. They use profits from their coffee sales to support a school and a library in the local farm community.

Since Trujillo's death, the Dominican Republic has moved toward democracy. "It's a different country now," Alvarez says. "The Dominican Republic has many dimensions. I've made connections with the real country, warts and all."

Like the characters in her stories and poems, Alvarez says she will always feel the

"I am a Dominican, *hyphen,* American."

tug-of-war between the cultures that claim her. "I am a Dominican, *hyphen*, American," she said in a 1994 interview. "As a writer, I find that the most exciting things happen in the realm of that hyphen—the place where two worlds collide or blend together."

"A novel is not, after all, a historical document, but a way to travel through the human heart," writes Julia Alvarez.

Julia Alvarez

Born:

March 27, 1950

Grew up:

Dominican Republic and New York

Life's work:

Poet, writer, and teacher

Website:

www.juliaalvarez.com

Favorite writers include:

Jane Austen, Emily Dickinson, Zora Neale Hurston, Maxine Hong Kingston (*The Woman Warrior* was a major influence), Toni Morrison, Alice Walker, Walt Whitman

Alvarez's works include:

Before We Were Free (novel)
How the García Girls Lost Their Accents (novel)
In the Name of Salomé (novel)
In the Time of the Butterflies (novel)
Once Upon a Quinceañera (nonfiction)
Return to Sender (novel)
Saving the World (novel)
The Woman I Kept to Myself (poetry)

She says:

"You read all these wonderful storytellers. After a while, you realize there's only one story you haven't heard—the one that only you can tell."

A Conversation with Author
John Shea

Q *What was your process for writing this book?*

A I did a lot of reading. I probably read every article and interview ever written about Sherman Alexie and Julia Alvarez. I also read works by both authors, especially their nonfiction books. Alvarez, in particular, has written essays about her life that were very helpful. I also interviewed her. Unfortunately, I wasn't able to talk to Alexie. His schedule made that impossible.

Q *Why is it so important to interview the people you're writing about?*

A You get to know them in a way that's impossible if all you have is their written work. You can hear their personality in their voice. You can ask them to confirm or deny any stories you've heard about them. Without that confirmation you have to rely on what other people have written about them.

Q *How do Alexie and Alvarez use writing as a way to define themselves?*

A Alexie didn't really start writing seriously until college. But he used writing to make sense of the different worlds he inhabited—rez kid and college student, alcoholic and poet. Writing helped him create his own tribe, as he might put it.

Alvarez was really at sea when she came to the United States. She found comfort and belonging in books. That extended to her writing. It helped her understand her new home and allowed her to reflect on her old home. It helped her live in both worlds and establish an identity as, in her words, "a Dominican, *hyphen*, American."

Q *What do these two writers have in common?*

A Each of them is seen as the voice of a community—even though they don't love being characterized that way. Alvarez writes about Dominican immigrants; Alexie writes about Native Americans, both on the reservation and off. The pictures they paint are not always flattering. Alexie's critics sometimes think he is making fun of Indians or highlighting their troubles instead of their accomplishments. Alvarez has had some similar difficulties. In the end, I think both create fully formed portraits of their worlds—both the good and the bad.

Q *Sherman Alexie does stand-up comedy in addition to writing poetry and fiction. Why is humor so important to him?*

A His stand-up comedy is part poetry slam and part shaggy dog storytelling [long, rambling stories]. His humor is dark. He may spend a half hour telling stories about drunkenness on the reservation. But in some ways, it seems that humor allows him to tackle tough subjects more easily. Sometimes uncomfortable subjects—death, drinking, discrimination—can best be handled with wit.

Q *Is there anything you learned about the two writers that you couldn't fit in the book?*

A Alexie has written a lot about how he and his father bonded over basketball. As a basketball fan—and a father—I could relate to that. I was also very interested in Alvarez's mother. She has worked with the United Nations to champion the rights of women and children in developing countries. From immigrant to parent to activist, she's lived a full life.

Q *Both Alexie and Alvarez felt like outsiders when they were young. How did that help shape them as writers?*

A Alexie was mercilessly teased for being small and nerdy. Later, when he went to the all-white Reardan High School, some rez kids called him an "apple"— red on the outside, white on the inside.

Alvarez left an idyllic life in the Dominican Republic for some cruel times in New York.

I think that being an "outsider" gave them each a chance to observe their worlds and write honestly about them. And let's not forget a more primal emotion—revenge. To some degree, both fantasized about being successful while their tormenters wallowed in mediocrity.

What to Read Next

Fiction

Cuba 15, Nancy Osa. (304 pages) *Violet manages to find the humor in preparing for a party she doesn't want—a traditional 15-year-old Cuban's quinceañera.*

The House on Mango Street, Sandra Cisneros. (110 pages) *A young Chicana woman tries to find a meaningful life growing up in Chicago.*

Indian Summer, Barbara Girion. (183 pages) *A young white girl eventually makes friends with the Indian girl she has to live with on a reservation.*

Rising Voices: Writings of Young Native Americans, Arlene Hirschfelder and Beverly Singer. (144 pages) *More than 60 poems and essays present the feelings of young Native American writers.*

The Way to Rainy Mountain, N. Scott Momaday. (98 pages) *Momaday uses the traditional stories and myths of his Kiowa ancestry to explore his own life.*

Nonfiction

The Rez Road Follies: Canoes, Casinos, Computers, and Birch Bark Baskets, Jim Northrup. (256 pages) *Northrup tells us about the present-day life of the Ojibway Indians with friendly humor.*

When I Was Puerto Rican, Esmeralda Santiago. (288 pages) *This is the story of the author's vibrant childhood in Puerto Rico and her family's emigration to the U.S.*

Books

The Absolutely True Diary of a Part-Time Indian,
Sherman Alexie. (288 pages) *This novel tells the story of Arnold Spirit Jr.—whose life happens to be very similar to Alexie's!*

Before We Were Free, Julia Alvarez. (192 pages) *A 12-year-old Dominican girl and her family live through the dangerous final years of Trujillo's dictatorship.*

Films and Videos

In the Time of the Butterflies (2001) *Alvarez's novel about the Mirabal sisters was adapted into a movie starring Salma Hayek and Edward James Olmos.*

Smoke Signals (1998) *Alexie wrote the screenplay for this movie, which was made by an all-Native American crew. It's based on stories from his book* The Lone Ranger and Tonto Fistfight in Heaven.

Websites

www.fallsapart.com
Alexie's site includes his biography and information about his movies, books, and recordings.

www.juliaalvarez.com
Alvarez's website gives information about her own work and the work of other people she admires.

education-portal.com/articles/40_of_the_Best_Websites_for_Young_Writers.html
This site has links to 40 great websites for young writers.

Glossary

alter ego (AWL-tur EE-goh) *noun* in literature, a character whose personality is similar to the author's personality

anatomy (uh-NAT-uh-mee) *noun* the study of the structure of living things

anthology (an-THOL-uh-jee) *noun* a collection of poems or stories by different writers that are printed in the same book

anticipation (an-TISS-i-pay-shuhn) *noun* the state of expecting something to happen and preparing for it

attribute (uh-TRIB-yoot) *verb* to credit someone for his or her work or words

borough (BUR-oh) *noun* one of the five political divisions of New York City: Brooklyn, the Bronx, Manhattan, Queens, and Staten Island

conspirator (kuhn-SPIHR-uh-tor) *noun* a person who makes secret, illegal plans with others

diligent (DIL-uh-juhnt) *adjective* hard-working and responsible

diplomat (DIP-luh-mat) *noun* a person who represents his or her country's government in a foreign country

elegy (EL-uh-jee) *noun* a sad poem or speech in memory of someone who has died

homogeneous (home-oh-JEE-nee-uhss) *adjective* composed of parts that are all very similar

hydrocephaly (hye-droh-SEF-uh-lee) *noun* an abnormal condition in which fluid collects around the brain. In infants it can cause the head to grow rapidly.

identity crisis (eye-DEN-ti-tee KRYE-siss) *noun* a personal conflict caused by confusion about the life one should live

introverted (IN-truh-vurt-ed) *adjective* shy; keeping one's thoughts and feelings to oneself

irreverent (i-REV-uh-ruhnt) *adjective* lacking respect for the beliefs of others

migrant (MYE-gruhnt) *adjective* moving from place to place, often in search of work

pigeonhole (PIJ-uhn-hohl) *verb* to think of someone or something in a specific and limited way

prejudice (PREJ-uh-diss) *noun* an unfair opinion about someone based on the person's race, religion, or other characteristic

realm (RELM) *noun* an area of interest; a world

regime (ri-ZHEEM) *noun* a government that rules a people for a specific period of time

reservation (rez-ur-VAY-shuhn) *noun* an area of land chosen by the U.S. government to belong to an Indian tribe

seizure (SEE-zhur) *noun* a sudden attack, spasm, or convulsion, caused by epilepsy or another disorder

smallpox (SMAWL-poks) *noun* a very contagious disease that causes chills, high fever, and blisters

stereotype (STER-ee-oh-tipe) *noun* an overly simple picture or opinion of a person, group, or thing

---

Metric Conversions

miles to kilometers: 1 mi is about 1.6 km

acres to hectares: 1 acre is about 0.4 hectares

Sources

NO RESERVATION

The Absolutely True Diary of a Part-Time Indian, Sherman Alexie. New York: Hachette Book Group, 2007. (including quotes on pages 4, 50, 53)

"The Absolutely True Interview with Sherman Alexie, an Amazing Part-Time Indian," Jesse Sposato. *Sadie Magazine,* Fall 2010. (including quote on page 30)

"All Rage and Heart," Maya Jaggi. *Guardian,* May 3, 2008.

"From Wellpinit to Reardan," Jim Blasingame. *ALAN Review,* Winter 2008. (including quote on page 26)

"An Indian Without Reservations," Timothy Egan. *New York Times,* January 18, 1998. (including quote on page 49)

"Interview with Sherman Alexie," Rita Williams-Garcia. National Book Foundation, 2007. (including quote on page 23)

The Lone Ranger and Tonto Fistfight in Heaven, Sherman Alexie. New York: Grove Press, 2005. (including quote on page 52)

"Man of Many Tribes," Sarah T. Williams. *Star Tribune,* December 31, 2007. (including quote on page 27)

"Sherman Alexie," by Joel McNally. *The Writer,* June 2001. (including quotes on pages 38–39)

"Sherman Alexie: A Reservation of the Mind," Doug Marx. *Publishers Weekly,* September 16, 1996. (including quotes on pages 25, 32, 42)

"Sherman Alexie Masks His Feelings but Not His Purpose," John Marshall. *Seattle Post-Intelligencer,* July 7, 1998.

"Spokane Words: Tomson Highway raps with Sherman Alexie." *Aboriginal Voices,* January–March 1997. (including quote on page 12)

"Superman and Me," Sherman Alexie. Milkweed Editions, August 26, 1997. (including quote on page 24)

"Talking with Sherman Alexie: Powwows and Pop Culture," by Liza Featherstone. *New York Newsday,* July 20, 2003. (including quotes on pages 39, 43)

The Top Ten: Writers Pick Their Favorite Books, J. Peter Zane. New York: W.W. Norton and Company, 2007.

"Trading Stories—From Life to Literature, on the Reservation," Donn Fry. *Seattle Times,* March 12, 1995. (including quotes on pages 16, 37, 38)

Understanding Sherman Alexie, Daniel Grassian. Columbia, SC: University of South Carolina Press, 2005.

WRITING HOME

Author's interview with Julia Alvarez in 2010. (including quotes on pages 59, 66, 67, 71, 76, 81, 82, 85, 86, 89, 91, 94, 97, 98, 101)

"About Me," Julia Alvarez. juliaalvarez.com. (including quotes on pages 76, 87)

"An American Childhood in the Dominican Republic," Julia Alvarez. *American Scholar*, Winter 1987. (including quotes on pages 70, 73)

Dominican Republic: A Country Study, edited by Richard A. Haggerty. Washington: Library of Congress, 1989.

"In the Name of Salomé: Julia Alvarez," Penguin Reading Guides. Penguin.com.

"In the Name of the Homeland," Hilary McClellen. *Atlantic Unbound*, July 19, 2000.

In the Time of the Butterflies, Julia Alvarez. Chapel Hill, NC: Algonquin Books, 1994. (including quote on page 100)

"Julia Alvarez." *Notable Hispanic American Women*, Book 2. Gale, 1998. (including quote on page 79)

"Julia Alvarez: Books that Cross Borders," Jonathan Bing. *Publishers Weekly*, December 16, 1996.

"Julia Alvarez: Real Flights of Imagination," Ben Jacques. *Americas*, January 2001.

Julia Alvarez: Writing a New Place on the Map, Kelli Lyon Johnson. Albuquerque, NM: University of New Mexico Press, 2005.

Latina Self-Portraits: Interviews with Contemporary Women Writers, Bridget Kevane and Juanita Heredia. Albuquerque: University of New Mexico Press, 2000. (including quote on page 63)

Latino Writers and Journalists, Jamie Martinez Wood. New York: Infobase Publishing, 2007.

"Las Mariposas," Ilan Stavans. *Nation*, November 1994. (including quote on pages 5, 99)

"Memory Is Already the Story You Made Up About the Past: An Interview with Julia Alvarez," Catherine Wiley. *Bloomsbury Review*, March 1992.

"Mixed Breed: A Profile of Julia Alvarez," Linda Simon. *The World and I*, November 1, 2002.

Outside the Law: Narratives on Justice in America, edited by Susan Richards Shreve and Porter Shreve. Boston: Beacon Press, 1997.

"Salon Mothers Who Think: Something to Declare," Dwight Garner. Salon.com, September 25, 1998.

Something to Declare, Julia Alvarez. New York: Penguin Group, 1999. (including quotes on pages 78, 92, 97)

"A Woman's Immigrant Experience," Christine Calvanese. Yale National Initiative.

Index